HER MOTHER'S EVIL CHOICE

EIGBE OSEMUDIAMEN MOSES

DEDICATION

I dedicate this book to my beloved parents, siblings, fiancee, all my readers and to the most high.

CONTENTS

PROLOGUE

My name is Samuel. I live in the South South region of my dear country Nigeria. I'm now in my early 80s. My niece's daughter Itohan often come over to lodge in my house anytime she and her husband have business to attend to in this region.   On one of such visit, I told her I was going to make a short book base on her story. She loved the idea and promise to keep a copy in her archive.

Her story is one that highlight the struggles life can unexpectedly plunge us into, the importance of not giving up hope, willingness to forgive and many more lessons.

CHAPTER 1

Growing up with her aunt, Itohan knew what the pit of hell looks like in literal terms. She barely know her father because her father died before she could even pronounce the word daddy. Her mother who was left with almost nothing, took her and her siblings to the village to stay with her aged parents and her younger sister while she try to get back on feet in the city. She assumed that her sister will take good care of her children since she and her husband where very kind to her while her husband was alive. Little did she know that she was making the worst assumption ever.

Being the last among three siblings, Itohan could have enjoyed cuddle, love and attention normally showered on last born. The turn of events in her early life denied her all of that. While staying with her grand parents, she enjoyed a glimpse of what love looked like when her grand father was alive. But upon his demise, her aunt became the emperor of their home as it were, and she ruled tyrannically. She will batter her young niece and nephew without any form of remorse. Whenever she set her eyes on them, the next thing she could think of is the next labour she will use them for. They knew nothing called rest, not even in the night. She will wake them up in the dead of night, around 3am to commence work. It is about this time sleep usually get deeper and dream set in. Itohan and her siblings could not even enjoy those blessings from nature.

She was able to struggle through her primary school when her grand father was still alive. At this time, her mother could send some money to be use for her children's schooling. But as you may guess, the money was never used for their schooling as her aunt diverted it for her personal use. Most time she spent the money on gift for her boy friend. The school bear with them for sometime after much pleading from neighbors and family friends with promises to pay up later. Later her mom find a way to be sending money without passing it through her sister since she don't use the money for what it is met for.

Growing up, Itohan and her siblings could only find

comfort in each others company, and sometimes with the children in the neighborhood as they sneak out to play with them. Whenever they are dealt with by their aunt, the eldest among them takes them aside and pet them, forgetting about his own pain. He sometimes offered to be flogged their own strokes of the cane in addition to his own. While they are being summoned to the farm, he will lead them there in the forest, do most of the work and carry the heaviest load home. Sometimes they do this while their mates are in the school learning. And sometimes they are pushed to go do some farm work as soon as they get back from school, no food no rest. With this kind of oppression or child labour as you may call it, it will be difficult for these children to do well in school, especially since they where just going into secondary school or college. This is their formative class to prepare them for more challenging courses ahead and eventually help them know which discipline to go for if they want to further their education into tertiary institution. Unfortunately, Itohan and her siblings spent these formative years forcefully doing farm work all day mostly on empty stomach.

Whenever her mom comes to visit them, they are strictly warned by their aunt not to mention anything about their maltreatment to her. But mothers will always hear silent voices of their children. She was able to infer that everything was not right with her children. She could have just carried them along with her to the city, but she herself is yet to find her feet there. So she choose to buy them a cheap GSM device with which she can be communicating directly with them. She placed it in the custody of the eldest. But he know very well if their aunt sees it, she will definitely cease it. So he decided to keep it with a friend and only go pick it up whenever they want to talk to their mother at a prearranged time. Their mother also find a way to be sending them some little money from time to time. This arrangement was everything for them as it helped them to some times eat out while returning from school, since as usual, they won't be allowed to eat at home until evening after they have returned from the farm.

As they where growing up, they found out ways to be making some money for themselves. Whenever children are needed to dance during cultural ceremonies, they volunteer to join and at the end of the day, they will be rewarded with some little token to motivate them. Also, they and some other children in the neighborhood go fetch wild vegetable and fruits whenever it is the season of such vegetables and fruits. They take them to the local market for sale. But the moment they get home their aunt is at the door waiting for them to come submit the money they made for the day. Of course if they refuse they know what will follow. So they decided to be keeping half of the money they make with a friend and submit the other half with the tyrant at home waiting for them. During these times, Itohan could recall some kind neighbors who will feed them along with their children and always encourage them not to give up, that someday they will be on their own as grown ups and won't be maltreated again.

CHAPTER 2

Few days ago, Itohan was reminiscing her childhood days as she was preparing her speech for the women summit to be held in Atlanta. She tried to rack her brain to figure out what could make an aunt to be so mean and cruel to her niece, nephew, sister and father. What could have caused the disconnection between she and her family members. For her aunt she reasoned: "Could it be that she and my mother where not in good terms right from time? But that cannot be. Mom do tell us about the happy times she and her sister do have together whenever she come visit her when my dad was alive. Or could it be that she was transferring the frustration of not finding a marriage mate on us, since almost all the boys she dated ended up leaving her? That cannot be the case also, because even when her relationship with her boy friend was going smoothly, she was still very mean to us." Her thought was interrupted when her phone rang. Yes she was in a five start hotel in an industrialize city to address women and young girls as part of her duty working with a world class organization whose aim is to provide support to vulnerable ones especially women. How did she come to be in this elevated position of travelling round the world? We will see as the story unfold.

Back in the village, things didn't improve much no matter how hard they try to please their aunt. In fact, they have to drop out of school as their grade kept dropping due to their absence from class most times. Their aunt became more brutal towards them and dominated her mother, Itohan's grand mother, to become mean to them also. It all came to a climax when Itohan's mother paid a surprise visit home to do something. She asked about her children and she was told that they have gone to the farm. She then asked them why her children are in the farm during school hours. She got to know the whole truth in the argument that ensued. The children came from the farm to meet heated argument at home. It was so intense that their belongings where thrown out through the window by their aunt and their grandmother. They where told to follow their mother to the city. Whereas neighbors and passersby try to intervene to make them take the children back in, Itohan and her siblings where not ready to take their belongings back into that house. With excitement as if the day of their redemption has finally arrive, they quickly took their bath as best as they can and got ready to leave with their mother, not minding what await them in the city.

CHAPTER 3

The city of Benin is located in the Southern part of Nigeria, the most populous country located in Africa. It is a beautiful city often renowned for its historic bravery before and during colonization. It's rich culture including their great sculptures and artifacts are known worldwide. The people are very lovely and welcoming. However it is not devoid of many problem bedeviling many cities in the world today which can range from heavy crime to high cost of living, to difficulty getting affordable accommodation. Despite these obvious challenges in the cities, there is still a continuous movement of many persons from the rural settlements to the city in search of a better life. That is the reason Itohan's parents moved over to the city few years before she was given birth to. They found a humble apartment to reside. They ventured into business immediately instead of joining the numerous people struggling to get employed in the few employment opportunities available. Her father started a shop where he sells provision. Things where progressing fine as he enjoys good patronage. All he required from his wife was to take care of the home and the child they had at that time and every other ones that will follow thereafter. Hence, Itohan's mother become a full time house wife. She never resented such position because she enjoyed taking care of their child and doing household chores. Although they where not having surplus riches, they where not lacking. They could afford their needs and also afford to host any family members that want to come for visit. This was the time Itohan's mother and aunt had a solid relationship as the later will always travel from the village to the city to spend time with her sister.

Few years after their third child, Itohan, was birthed, her parents decided to look into some other businesses, since the proceed from the provision shop can hardly carter for the ever increasing need of their expanding family. They decided that transportation business would be fine. So Itohan's father got a car on hire and was using it for taxi within the city, leaving the shop for a sales girl under the supervision of his wife. How they wished that they have eyes to see into the future and know that this line of business would plunge them into misery!

The day dawned normal on one of the Fridays of July 1999. Workers started coming out to get taxi to take them to work. All those who have somewhere going started coming out to get taxi. Early morning like this and late afternoons after the workers have closed from work, are the best time for taxi drivers. So on this morning, as Itohan's father was about to go start the business of the day, little did he know that it is the last time he will set his eyes on his beautiful family. Little did he know that he will go out from them and not return to them again. If he had know, he would have hug his wife so dearly as never before, he would have carried little Itohan who was not up to three years at that time in his bosom and not let go of her, he would have cuddled his children as he has never done before. In fact, if he had known, he would have stayed home that day. The news of the fatal accident he was involved in that day reached his wife amid disbelieve. She rushed to the hospital where the accident victims where taken to and there it was, her greatest fear has happened. Her dear one laid lifeless on the hospital bed where doctors tried to revive him. His body was injured all over and bloodied. "I can't survive this" she cried. "My backbone, my sole confidant, my only friend and husband is gone. Who will I run to and who will always be there for me?" If tears could bring back the living, she was willing to cry an ocean of tears to have him back alive.

The days following the burial where never the best for Itohan's mother and her children as her late husband's family members offered them everything but comfort. They came to stripe the house and the shop off everything valuable claiming it belongs to their son. She took up courage to go meet them to negotiate with them how they can render support for the up keep of their son's children. The only thing they gave her was insults, threat not to come again and accusation that she killed their son. Going to the authority would have been fine for her, but you need to have some money to pursue cases like this at that time. And most of the time, the matter may take unnecessarily long to get settled and you may not even get what you are looking for. So what can she do at this moment except to take the children to her own parents to take care of, while she try to get back on her feet again. This is how Itohan and her siblings found themselves in their mother's village. They enjoyed some love and affection when their grand father was alive. But after he died some years later, all hell was let loose on them by their aunt who also turned their grand mother against them. The later who once saw them as beloved came to despise them. Their aunt do mercilessly give them up to 25 strokes of the cane over normal children's mistake such as weeing on their pants. The day she will have mercy on them, she will rather make them drink their urine instead of flogging them. But now that they are going back to the city with their mother, to them old things have pass away. New life and new things is what they hope for and look forward to. But new challenges will surface as well. Time will reveal what these challenges will be and how they will deal with them.

CHAPTER 4

Getting to their mother's single room apartment stuffed with all her properties, they could get a glimpse of the life their mother has been living, a life of struggle that is far from luxurious. Despite that, they will prefer to struggle under their mothers care than to be use as slaves by their aunt.

After some time has passed, their mother could afford to send them to a close-by public school. Itohan was 15 by now and she was to resume first year in Junior secondary school. She will have to deal with ridicule from her classmates who do not need to be told that Itohan was too old for that class. At 15, one suppose to be in senior secondary class under normal circumstances. How Itohan wished that her classmates knew her exact situation in life which is far from normal! But against all odds, Itohan was determine to overlook any side talk from her classmates met to discourage her. She was determine to fulfill her dream of pursuing her education as far as university level, and working in an organization where she can be useful in helping vulnerable ones. What she went through in the hands of her aunt impress on her young mind that there are many children all over the world that needs someone to speak for them and rescue them. She was determine to do her best to be that person. With much persuasion, the principal allowed her to resume Junior class after listening to how she and her siblings have not been so opportune to concentrate on their studies while in the village. Haven made up her mind not to pay attention to whatever mockery her classmates will spill on her, she soon got use to their talks and even made friends with some of them.

Being a teenager, her female features were becoming more prominent. Her facial beauty becomes more and more undeniably obvious. This opened up a new wave of unexpected pressure for her that almost made her gave up on humanity.

It all started one day when Mr. Joseph her Maths teacher called her aside after he had a class with them. He told her that the entire staff has noticed that she is very clever and they are always proud of her. She was obviously blushing at such encomium being showered on her. Mr. Joseph went further to tell her to try spare 15 minutes of her break time to come help him mark some scripts in the staff room. She innocently agreed and was even glad to be extended such privilege which every student look forward to. Whenever she goes into the staff room to help him, other staff present always praise her not just for her intelligence but for being well behaved as well. To her, these seems to confirm the genuineness of what Mr. Joseph told her before. She was always helping Mr. Joseph to enter the scores of other students into the continuous assessment sheet just as he showed her how to do it. The praises Mr. Joseph do shower on her gradually turn into attempt to be touching her in subtle manner. This time she started to doubt the true intention of this teacher whom seemed to be giving her more and more attention and always crave her company at any slightest opportunity. She became more cautious with him. His true intention finally came to the fore when he told her that he will need to spend more time with her privately. And then he told her to make it over to his place on Saturday of that week. Out of shock, she quickly interrupted him with questions; "Why privately? Why

Saturday?" Before she could blow out more questions, he interrupted her also and assured her that everything will be fine, that she should just make time to come. She was dump founded and lost in thought as she try to fathom what could be the real reason behind the invite she just received. She didn't even noticed when the teacher left. She only came back to her senses when her friend Juliet came to tap her shoulder when she didn't respond while she was calling her. As they both walked to their classroom, Juliet asked her why she was so deep in thought. She simply told her not to border, that it was nothing serious.

Meanwhile, some other male students where also after her. The most noticeable among them was Elvis. She know Elvis very well because he was so popular in the school as a notorious bully in the senior class. He has been punished several times for beating up fellow students who don't yield to his demand. It seems the school management has even run out of option on how to handle Elvis since he has not been found wanting to the extent of deserving rustication. Elvis wanted Itohan to befriend him. So he walked up to her one of the days and told her in the presence of her friend Juliet that he want her to be his girl friend, that even if she refuse, he always have a way of getting what he wanted. He told her that he was giving her two weeks to consider his request and then he walked away. Bewildered, Juliet asked her how she came in contact with this guy. Obviously shivering due to the treat, Itohan manage to answer her friend and told her that she has never had any contact with him until few minutes ago. Her fear became more obvious when Juliet went on to tell her the havoc Elvis has wrecked on the school. Even some teachers has had a fair share of his trouble as he do waylay them if they dare stand on his way.

At the close of school that day, she could barely walk home as she became so exhausted not from school activities, but from thinking. She had a lot going through her mind at the same time. First it is Mr. Joseph's invitation and now Elvis's threat. Of course she has been getting a lot of comment about her beauty from males, but non of them has come with these kind of out-front she is getting now. When she got home, her obvious exhaustion was dismissed by her mother to be due to her school activities and the scourging heat of the sun under which they walked home. So she simply told her to go get a cool shower and take a rest. Itohan just decided to watch event unfold and not tell her mother anything yet.

The Saturday Mr. Joseph invited her over came and gone. Itohan made up her mind not to pass through his street, talk less of going to his house. When school resumed the following Monday, she pretended as if nothing happened. After concluding his class with them, he called her aside as usual and led her to a safe distance from the classroom so that other curious student will not hear what he is about to say. He asked her why she did not come over to his place on Saturday. She said she couldn't come because she did not understand why he wanted to have private time with her. Appearing more desperate now, he told her to make sure she didn't disappoint him next Saturday again, that he want to see her in his house. Itohan respectfully told him not to expect her because she won't come. Wanting to explode like a time bomb and trying to restrain himself at the same time, he was sweating all over. He rain all kinds of threats on her. He told her he will continue to make sure she fail his subject as long as she refuse to honour his invitation and that he will make life miserable for her in the school. Knowing the importance of Maths to her progress educationally, she cannot afford to perform poorly in Maths. However, that was not enough to make her bow to Mr. Joseph's cravings.   As   she   now decided to speak out to her friend Juliet, she was about to receive the greatest shock of her life. During   time   for recess, she told Juliet about the invitation Mr. Joseph extended to her, how she refuse and the threat she received from him. Not looking surprise, Juliet told her that everyone know that Mr. Joseph is that type of a man who sleep around with his students not minding whether they are minor. Itohan getting angry, asked why no body has reported him to the school authority. Juliet told her that she don't know but all she know is that Mr. Joseph always carry out his threat, that the students he sleep with may be afraid he will carry out the threat he may have threatened them after the act. What shocked her the most is what Juliet told her next, that some students believe that Mr. Joseph has also slept with her.

Till she got home that day, the statements; "Mr. Joseph

always carry out his threat," and "some students think that he has also slept with her," refuse to get off her mind. She made up her mind to finally tell her mother everything and nip off the problem at its bud, before all those that has threatened her starts carrying out their threat.

CHAPTER 5

She was in for another big surprise as she approach her mother to talk to her when they where both alone at home in the evening. She started with the most desperate of them Mr. Joseph. She narrated to her mother everything that has transpired between she and her maths teacher. Before she could start narrating that of her school mate, Elvis, her mother interrupted her, asking why she didn't tell her about it all these while. She paused Elvis part and answered her mother, telling her that she never knew Mr. Joseph could descend so low to do such a thing. Her mother proceeded to tell her that if she had known about the whole thing right from the on set, she wouldn't have allowed her to react the way she reacted. That she would have allowed her to go see the teacher in his house. Itohan quickly blot out: "What if he also succeeded in sleeping with me just as he is alleged to have done to some other students?" Her mother told her that it would have been a problem if Mr. Joseph had slept with her and not given her a reasonable amount of money. Itohan who is still in disbelieve about what she just heard from her mother, adjusted and sat down properly and asked her mother if she is serious about what she just said. Her mother then went on to narrate to her how she has been surviving after her father's death. She said she do give in to the advances of some men to get whatever she wants. She told her that she was able to secure her present job after she gave in to the advances from the manager of that film. She further told her that her own approach to life is, use whatever you have to get whatever you want. At this time tears started rolling out of Itohan's eyes as she comes to discover that her mother does not have the solution she wanted. In an angry mood, she shouted at her mother asking her: "Whatever happened to dignity? Should you just throw it away for some gains? Am I no longer a minor?" When the mother heard her last question, she replied in a stronger tone saying: "You are only a minor in your heart. You stop being so the day you tell yourself otherwise. That is why I love your sister. She has been doing well making some money for the home!" At this point her mouth was wide open and she couldn't close it back. She was once again frozen in thought, thinking: "Why did she say she love my sister, what does she mean that she has been doing well making some money for the home?" She will later learn that her sister has slept with some teachers and even some neighbors for a huge amount of money with the consent of her mother.

At this point, Itohan was no longer thinking about anything that has to do with her school again. She has made up her mind to stop school if it comes to that, rather than consent to sleeping around with a teacher or a fellow student. Now she spent her time thinking about how quickly she and her siblings has grown apart. Instead of having each others back and finding comfort in each others company as it was back then in the village when they where younger, they barely know each other now. Her brother who once offered to receive strokes of cane on their behalf is now very hostile to them, as he spends most of his time with the boys in the neighborhood who are notorious for bad behavior. He beats them a lot and never find anything good in whatever they do. And right now, she does not know what is going on in her sister's life. "What happened?" She asked herself. "Could it be growth or a side effect of trying to survive in the city?" No matter what is responsible, what she just discovered about she and her siblings relationship is something that will continue to give her sleepless night. She could only wish she could bring back the good old days.

CHAPTER 6

It was all too easy for the staffs in the school to know that Itohan is now a shadow of herself. She no longer wears the smile she was known for, and also her performance in almost all subject has dropped drastically. The principal decided to call her to his office and find out what is going on with her. As she walked to the principal's office, she refuse to bother herself about the possible reasons the principal wanted to see her.   After answering her knock and inviting her to have her seat, the principal narrated to her how the whole school has been proud of her performance and welcoming nature. But that lately, there has been a great drift in her performance and countenance. He then told her to pour out her heart to him so that he can offer some help. She couldn't stop biting her finger out of apprehension and confusion if solution can actually come from the principal. The principal kept assuring her of his readiness to assist. Finally tears started to roll down her cheek. At this time, the principal started thinking that it must be an emotional problem. So he called in one of the female staff and told her to take Itohan aside to a lonely place and find out what is wrong with her.

After listening carefully to everything Itohan has to say, the teacher came back to the principal's office with a frown face as if she has just seen a ghost. She then reported everything to the Principal. He once again reassured Itohan that he will get to the root of the matter so that she can be free from harassment. Itohan thanked him and the female teacher, and then she was excused. The principal know exactly what to do. As the school don't tolerate such conduct from teachers, he quickly called in the vice principal so that they can look into the matter quickly. They both listened to the female teacher again as the principal told her to repeat what Itohan told her. After that he excused her so that he can deliberate on the matter with the vice. They decided to set up a committee to investigate what the teacher has been alleged to have done. If found wanting, Mr. Joseph will loose his job in the school and will be handled over to the appropriate authority since some of the students in question are minors. Then for the student Elvis, the principal knows that Mr. Sunday, the teacher all the students dread the most, will be enough to handle that. He called Mr. Sunday and explained everything to him and instructed him on what to do.

The next day Mr. Sunday called Itohan to his office. After she came, he sent someone to also call Elvis to his office. When he was told that Mr. Sunday want to see him in his office, he knew that there is fire on the mountain. With his tail tucked between his legs, he came into Mr. Sunday's office. Then Mr. Sunday asked him if he knew Itohan. He said yes, that she is a student of the school also. Then the teacher asked him who gave him the audacity to threaten her for refusing to be his girl friend. He denied even talking to her, talk less of threatening her. Then the teacher told him that it is high time they put a stop to his waywardness in the school. He told Elvis that if Itohan ever report that anybody dares to threaten her again, beat her or even insult her, he would be held accountable for it. He was made to sign an undertaken to this effect after which he was assign to cut some grasses as punishment. After that day, instead of being a terror to Itohan, he became a guardian to her by always watching her back to make sure no body mistreat her. Base on what he signed with Mr. Sunday, he knows that he will be held accountable and could face severe punishment if anybody maltreat Itohan.

After some weeks passed, the principal called Itohan back to his office because he was not done with her yet. The last time he thought about her, he told himself that, this pretty, intelligent and innocent girl surely needs someone to be guiding her. If not, she can easily fall prey to those predators in men who use money or anything attractive to lure young girls after them. That she was fortunate in Mr. Joseph's case, but may not be so fortunate next time especially since growth and changes in her body will soon be adding to the pressure.

When Itohan got to his office, he asked her how things has been with her since the last time she came to his office. She said things has been fine, that she don't get any harassment anymore, and she thanked him for helping her out. The principal told her that even if the larger part of the society may be corrupt, there is still a small section of it that refuse to be corrupted, that she can always find help in this section. So he further told her that anytime she has any burden on her, instead of trying to bear it alone, she should always come to him, that he will always try to offer necessary solution. Then he told her that the main reason he called her was to discuss with her what her mother told her. He told her that tough situation in life can greatly distort the way someone view things. Such may be the case with her mother. Probably after the death of her husband, she was stranded. Having little children to take care of, she gave in to whatever a corrupt society has to offer and with time, it became normal to her. He greatly impress in her that it is not proper to always use whatever one has to get whatever one want as her mother has told her. There are some things that one has that is worth keeping, one of them being ones dignity. It should never be traded for anything, else, you will become like a mere rag before people. He advice her not to imbibe the ancient ideology that a woman don't need to be skilled since she will be taken care of by her husband when she get married. This idea has led many women to be stranded with little or no choice if their husband dies. He encouraged her to start preparing herself to pursue any carrier of her choice.

After encouraging her with many words and advice, he then told her what he has planned. He told her that henceforth, Miss Helen, the female teacher she confided in, has been appointed to personally look after her. He advice her to always open up to her and feel free to always approach her for help. Itohan thanked the principal so much for his fatherly care and promised that she will hearken onto his words. After that the principal called in Miss Helen and told her to take Itohan with her so that they could rub minds together.

CHAPTER 7

The day she graduated from secondary school was such a joyous day for Itohan. Being the best graduating student among the art students, she was given so many gifts. She was showered plenty praises by both staffs and parents alike. Almost all fellow students wanted to be photographed with her. She surely felt on top of the world that day. After Many days passed, she still can't put down the photos she snapped on her graduation day as she frequently bring them out to look at. It was on one of these occasion when she was watching her photos that her mother came to her with another surprise.

Her mother asked her what her plan was, since it is more than a month since she graduated from secondary school. She told her mother that her plan was to find a place to learn how to bake, pending when she will be able to go into the university to study guidance and counseling. Her mother told her that learning how to bake won't be necessary that she can start seeking admission into the university immediately. Excited, but confuse, she asked her mother how she will manage to finance her through the university alone. That she should be allowed to learn baking first, so that she can be contributing to her university finances. Her mother told her that the man that owns one of the biggest shopping mall in their area has been expressing interest to marry her ever since she was 16, but that she told him to be patient until she finish secondary school before the whole arrangement can be perfected. She further told Itohan that since she is now 20, she don't see anything that should hold her back from marrying the man. To further convince her, she told Itohan that the man is not only ready to sponsor her through the university immediately, but he will also buy her the latest car, take her outside the country for vacations as often as possible and be financially responsible for her siblings and mother. Itohan sounding not so surprise because she has come to know the way her mother view things, told her that she will not marry the man because she is not ready to be a second wife. She told her mother that if at all the man is single, that she cannot afford to marry someone she don't know. To her mother's amazement, she told her that she is already in love with a boy called Efe. Her Mother raised her voice angrily and asked her; "Who is Efe?" She replied; "The mechanic boy down the street!" Her mother sounding a note of warning, told Itohan: "Cancel whatever feeling you have for that penniless boy whose parents cannot even afford two square meals a day, and start considering marrying the man who will better our lot in life." She left the house after sounding this note of warning and Itohan felt unconcern because there is nothing that can make her marry a man who already has children, one of whom is almost her age mate.

Later that day, when it got to the time they agreed to be meeting, Itohan went to see Efe in the workshop where he works. She told him everything that transpired between she and her mother earlier that day. He consoled her by telling her that if she refuse to shift her ground, her mother will consent to her wish and stop disturbing her about marrying someone she is not willing to marry. He further promised to always be there for her. As they where spending the little time they have together as best as they can before Efe resume his work, her mother was looking at the workshop intently as she was passing by. She was trying to catch sight of Efe as she couldn't fathom how on earth he was able to get the attention of her daughter Itohan. She was surprised when she finally saw, not just Efe but Itohan obviously enjoying Efe's company because she was just laughing out as they where talking together. She quickly changed direction from going home. She went straight to Efe's mother's shop. There she warned her to tell her son to stay away from her daughter, else she will give them the trouble they are looking for. Before Efe's mother could speak out, she turned back and left.

After some days passed, Itohan's mother came to ask her if she has consider meeting the man she told her about. She told her that she has nothing to consider because the man is not her choice. She shouted at her and asked her why can't she be like her sister for once. That her sister do bring home some money, but that she only knows how to eat whereas she brings home nothing. Itohan quickly reminded her that if she starts learning how to bake, in a short while she will also be in a position to be bringing something home. Her mother told her that the chicken change she will be able to bring from baking will not be enough for anything. Now appearing persuasive, she told Itohan that she can be in love with anyone she want to, but she should just date this man for some time and get somethings from him. Itohan told her that it won't be fair to Efe, that she is not ready to cheat on him. Her mother then told her that she knows what to do and then left angrily. Itohan went to meet her sister to really find out everything her mother always says about her. From the conversation they had, though an unfriendly conversation, she was able to find out that her sister is fond of jumping from one rich guy to another. If any guy give her the slightest green light, she is willing to abandon the present guy she is dating for the new one if the new one is richer. Itohan told her that such life style is not befitting non profitable. Her sister strictly told her that everyone has their own life to live. That if she choose to live hers that way, it is non of her business. That she should never come to discuss anything about her life with her again. Itohan could clearly see why her mother is very proud of her sister, she is living the way she want her to live.

Her mother didn't miss words when she told her that she knows what to do. Her mother was now determine to make life more miserable for her. First her mother and her sister refuse to let her have dinner that evening, telling her that she will start eating the day she starts bringing money home. She survived on whatever they left over. They will constantly make jest of her and purposely say things that will annoyed her very much. At this time their brother is no longer staying with them and he seldom visit. Probably he would have been able to put a stop to all these maltreatment.

Not knowing what to do next, Itohan went back to

her school to see her principal. Her principal was so happy to see her after so many months. He ask her about her welfare, then Itohan told him everything she has been going through at home. Feeling very sorry for her, the principal told her he will try to come in to help. He send words to her mother and she finally came after several days of excuses because she never wanted to come to see the principal. She knew that the principal must asked about Itohan in addition to any other topic he want to discuss with her. Hardily did she know that Itohan's welfare is the only subject they will discuss.

The principal welcome her very well and made her feel at home. After asking about her welfare and that of the family at large, he went further to tell her that the girl child is very important to the family not because they can cut corners to make the family rich with what they have, but that they can project the family to unimaginable height if the family invest on their intelligence by way of educating them and dignifying them by allowing them make their own choices in life. He told her that Itohan is such an intelligent girl that should be educated as far as possible. And he told her that the record Itohan set in the school is yet to be broken. After they spoke at length, the woman thanked her and left.

She rushed home panting and obviously angry. Itohan's sister was at home and she asked her mother what the problem was. Her mother invited her to sit down, that the situation in the house has taken a new dimension. The sister sat down and told her mother to explain what she meant. Her mother told her that Itohan has gone about reporting them to different people, that she is just coming from the principal's office. And then she narrated everything the principal told her. Angrily, Itohan's sister told her mother that they should not allow Itohan to sleep in the house that night, that she should go and pass the night where ever she like. When Itohan got home that day, she was surprise that her mother and sister refuse to open the door for her to come inside. Her sister came out to tell her that since she has made up her mind to be narrating them about, she will not sleep in that house that night. She asked her sister how and when it happened, and who she narrated them to. Her sister simply locked the door behind her. She waited around thinking that they will change their mind and open the door for her. After waiting long hours and it was getting to about 11pm, she decided to go to one of their family friends house located some distance from their house. She went there alone in the dead of night. On reaching there, she knocked and knocked and knocked, but there was no response. It was obvious that she has gone to sleep. Itohan then sat in an area close to the door and that is where she slept till day break. When the lady came out and saw her there, she fearfully asked; "Who is that?" Itohan yawned and replied "It is me Itohan." She quickly invited her in and after Itohan told her how she came to be at her door in the middle of the night, she was dump founded. She took her phone and called Itohan's mother. In strong terms, she told Itohan's mother how wrong her action was no matter the provocation that caused it. She took Itohan back home and repeated to Itohan's sister and mother what she said on the phone.

Things went on like this for a long time until Efe felt he could not take it any longer. He told Itohan that he cannot stand seeing her being maltreated because of him. He pointed out several occasions her mother chase her on the street yelling to her to stop associating with him, many times she has been locked out of the house. He also mention several other inhuman treatment she has endured because of him. He told her that if he was the one bearing the brunt, it would have been easier. So he suggested that they go apart in the main time and see what the future holds. Difficult though it was, she saw reasons with what Efe said and they both agreed to stay away from each other for now. Knowing that just staying away from Efe will not really solve the problem, Itohan has to make definite plan for herself because she wasn't ready to live her life the way her mother wanted. When her mother got to notice that her relationship with Efe wasn't tight anymore, she was no longer hostile at home. She thought that with time Itohan will yield to her request.

CHAPTER 8

Itohan wanted to use this period of relative calm to equip herself so that she can reduce her dependence on those who don't want her good. She went to meet her principal and told him how things have 'improved' since he spoke with her mother last. The principal asked her why she didn't come over to report to him that things deteriorated. She said she simply did not want to bother him too much. She told him that she has planned to reduce her dependence on them so that they will not be using that as a wedge against her anymore. She further explained to him that she want to use few months to learn how to bake but that she don't have the money needed to get the training. The principal asked her how much it will cost and gave it to her when she told him. He also told her to come to him if she need further assistance. She told the principal how grateful she was for his relentless and unconditional support. As soon as she started learning the skill, she quickly got the mastery of everything to the amazement of her tutors. They told her that some people do spend more than 6 months and they will still not grasp the basics. That they are amaze that within one month she has learned very far. They freely left her to bake even delicate once for their customers and this further accelerated her learning process. By the time she has spent the agreed 6 months, she has master everything about baking and how to handle customers request and ensure timely delivery. After allowing such a longtime to pass, her mother thought she will be ready to agree to her request to at least date the man he told her about and get some monetary and material gift from him. Also the man is pressuring her for her daughter more than ever. She approach Itohan once more and Itohan made it clear to her that she will never have anything to do with that man. She then told Itohan to pack her things and go away from her house. She found it unbelievable that her mother will drive her away from her house. She was convinced that she was not dreaming, when her mother repeated to her that she don't want to see her in her house by the time she returns home in the evening. Itohan quickly reached out to the film where she learned her skills and asked them if they have vacancy. They told her yes, that one of the bakers have just left, that she should come immediately for them to discuss her employment condition if she needed employment. When she got there she asked them if they offer accommodation. They said yes, but it is reserve for those that come from a far distance. Itohan told them that she will really need to be accommodated there even though her place is not so far off. They consulted with those in charge of the accommodation and offer it to her since no body was using it at the moment. Itohan couldn't thank her God enough who solved her problem of work and accommodation in a sitting.

CHAPTER 9

The moment Itohan started working with the film, she called her brother to brief him about what has happened. She told him how she was driven out of the house by their mother and sister. His brother promised to get back to her after reaching their mother. He called their mother to ask why she drove her own daughter out of her house. She lied that Itohan has turned wayward and have started insulting her. He told her that those where not enough reasons to drive her out. He called Itohan back to ascertain if she really insulted her, she said no. Her brother said he knows that their mother was lying, but that she should apologize to her so that there will be peace. Itohan told him no problem, that she will do anything within her power to make peace reign.

She called her mother after work that day and told her she is sorry if she ever insulted her. Her mother said she accept her apology. Her relationship with her mother turn a new leaf as her mother kept calling to check on her every other day.

But one day Itohan's sister who was still living at home with her mother told her mother that she is worried about something. Her mother told her to open up to her whatever it is that is disturbing her. She told her mother that she is worried that Itohan will be narrating them about, telling everyone the way they live their lives. Her mother told her that it is possible but that they cannot do anything about it. Itohan's sister told her that there is something that they can do. She suggested to her mother that, they should invite Itohan home under the pretence that there are some urgent matters they want to discuss as a family. And then they will beat her up and threaten her never to discuss the situation of their lives with no one. Her mother grudgingly accepted and then Itohan's sister put a call across to Itohan. Itohan agreed to come over in the evening. Despite agreeing to her sister over the phone, Itohan don't really want to go because she thinks that they want to start persuading her again to date the man her mother told her about.

When it was evening and she was not forthcoming, her sister called her again, and Itohan told her that she cannot make it because she is still at work. At this point,

Itohan's sister told her mother that they should go meet her at her work place and beat her there. They took taxi and on getting to the premises, they worked into the customer's section of the film and they met Itohan attending to some customers. Thinking they are there to get some things, Itohan's colleague came to them to ask them what they wanted. They told them they came to see Itohan. So they where shown where to sit down and wait for her. As soon as Itohan finished with her customers, she went to meet them. Before she could say a greeting, her sister slapped her and her mother did same. She retaliated by returning her sister's slap and a fight ensued. As people around try to separate them from fighting, her mother was just shouting and saying that enough is enough for Itohan, that she do go about telling people that she, her mother, and her elder sister are prostitute. After managing to douse the tension, the security men sent her mother and her sister away. The manager called Itohan to her office and asked her who those people are. She told the manager that they are her family members. The manager did not believe. She asked her; "Are you sure that woman is your mother?" Itohan told her yes.

After telling her that she can't believe that a mother can afford to fight her daughter in public, she warned her that if such family issue interfere with her work again, she will be relieved of her duty. Itohan told her she understand, and she apologized. After that she was told to close for the day to go put herself together.

Itohan couldn't sleep that night. She was just thinking what could have prompted them to come fight with her in public. She kept thinking: "When did our family situation deteriorated to this extent? When and who did I tell that my mother and my sister are prostitute?" She thought she can never bear the shame and embarrassment this brought to her. She still manage to put herself together and report to work daily and gradually, she got over the whole thing.

Miss Helen called her one of these days while she was at work. She told Itohan to come over to her place during the weekend because she have something important to discuss with her. On getting to her place, Miss Helen who is now married, asked about her welfare. Itohan replied: "My evil mother has made me pass through a lot." Then she went further to relate what her mother and sister has done to her recently. Miss Helen assured her that they cannot do worst than that. She also told her that very soon all those harassment will stop. Then she told her the reason why she called her. She told her that her husband said that they are looking for vibrant young girls in their organization. That even though the person have not attained a university degree, she could be accepted and then if she is diligent with her duty, she could be sponsored to the university by the company. Itohan did not waste time to tell her that she is interested. So miss Helen told her that when her husband arrive from London the following week, she will discuss further with him and if possible invite her over to speak with her husband.

Weeks later, after she confirmed that she was among those that where successfully employed, she tendered her resignation letter to the film she was working with as a baker. They organized a sent forth party for her and they told her she will be greatly missed. They prayed for her and wished her success in her future endeavors.

She was able to secure a little apartment close to

the company she is now working with as there was no arrangement at that moment to take them into their staff quarters. After working with them for two years, the company shortlisted her among the staffs that will be sponsored to the university. They will be allowed to study any discipline of their choice that will be useful to the company. Good enough, graduates of guidance and counseling are among those useful to the company. This has been Itohan's dream course of study. At the age of 25, Itohan was finally able to secure admission into the university to study her dream course.

Due to the fact that Itohan's relationship with her mother and elder sister has deteriorated more after they came to fight her, they don't know much about Itohan anymore. They hardly talk on phone, Itohan don't go visiting them, in fact the few times they talked over the phone, their conversation merely reduce to just exchanging greetings. Because of this, they don't know how much Itohan has progressed in life. They still think that she is working as a baker.

Itohan struggle to do her best in her course despite the tight schedule of combining school and work together.

She was doing well in her studies and her place of work. She purposely decided not to inform her mother that she has been admitted into the university until the day she graduate. When the day of her graduation finally came, she called her mother that morning and told her that she was graduating from the university that day. Her mother was surprised and ask her how she did it. She told her mother to help her thank her God who made everything possible, and told her that she will explain more next time. She invited her for their graduation ceremony that was scheduled to hold on the weekend at the company's event center.   When her mother told her sister about the exciting news she got that day, her sister simply asked her what is exciting about that. Then her mother mockingly told her that its exciting because its a sign that Itohan is progressing unlike her that has refuse to progress in life and still lives under her roof. Not wanting to be mocked that day, which has become common with her mother lately, she just walked away from her presence.

Few years later after Itohan attained her university qualification. Now the company was set to promote her and some other staff. But before they perfect such promotion, they usually make those to be promoted to get some training in the position they will be promoted to. So they assign Itohan to always go with one of the female executive member on her trips to carry out the company's assignment, because very soon, this will be one of Itohan's official assignment. It was one of those trip with her boss that brought Itohan to Atlanta. While she spent her time in her hotel room thinking why her family relationship deteriorated so much, it was her boss' call that interrupted her thought. She called Itohan to remind her certain things to put into consideration while delivering her speech before the audience gathered to hear them. Her Boss affirmed to the company that Itohan has always been doing well with her parts and that she is good to go for the position. The company promoted her to that position and granted her all the benefits that comes with it. These benefit include but not limited to, having an SUV as her official car, moving into the company's quarter for senior staffs, several allowances and a mouth watery take home salary at the end of the month.

When Itohan and all the other staffs that where promoted got the notification, there was jubilation all over the place.

Her first official assignment as an executive member was to speak to some men, women and children at a refugee camp in one disaster ravaged country. She decided to use the lessons of her life to conclude her speech with them. She said: "Even though everything life present to you is telling you that you are not worthy to fulfill your dreams, don't let go. Hold on to your dreams and let them be your motivation. Take charge of your life and do not let any situation push you to let go off your values and principles. Don't feel too big to take advantage of smaller opportunities around you, these could be stepping stones to fulfilling your dreams. Above all, accept help from those who genuinely want to help you, don't see it as a let down."

When recalling all the blessings she has received, meeting Raymond was the most exciting. Raymond is a mechanical engineer working with a renowned construction company. He is a gentle man in his 30s. At a time, he was lodged in the same hotel with Itohan when he came to oversee some work his company was handling in that vicinity. The first time they met in the Hotel reception, they couldn't stop staring at each other. Raymond made a move to exchange contact with her and they have always been communicating since then. They have visited each other several times and are planning to make the next move.

Haven worked for some years now, Itohan now has plans that she will like to unveil to her family members. So she called her mother and informed her that she will be coming over during the weekend. Her mother promised to wait for her at home. When she got there, everybody came to greet her and tell her how different she looked. In the evening while she was with her mother and her sister, she told them that she planned to get two piece of land in that area. She will built a befitting house for her mother on one of them and build a shopping plaza on the other one for her mother to be in charge of. And she also told them about Raymond and promised to bring him home soon to see them. Her mother and sister tearfully rained prayers and good wishes on her. When she was alone the next day, her mother approach her to beg her to help her sister secure any job position where she work. She smiled and told her that she has a different plan for her sister. That she has told her sister that it is necessary for her to travel abroad to start a new life. And that she will sponsor her trip and assist her over there till she regain her feet. She told her that her sister agreed to the plan but insisted that she will not leave until after Itohan's marriage. Her mother hugged her and confess that she is a blessing to the family.

Itohan will not spend the weekend without going to see the principal. On her way there she decided to stop by Efe's workshop. She was told that Efe has stopped working with them some years back because he moved to Lagos. They gave her his new phone contact and she promised to reached him.

On getting to the principal's house, she was shocked to see that he was seriously ill. Her beloved principal could hardly talk because he was so weak. She asked his wife and those around what the problem was. They told her that some years back, he was diagnose of diabetes, that he has been following up with check up, taking his medications and following their recommendation for his meal. But that lately, he could not go for checkup non buy his medicine due to their unpaid salary for six months now. So he could not even follow his special meal recommended for him. All these made his health deteriorate further. Itohan did not waste time to arrange for him to be taken to one of the specialist hospital in the city. She use her car to convey him there herself and told the doctor to give him prompt attention. She paid all the money they demanded and she gave more money to his wife to take care of further expenses that may arise. She promise to call everyday to check on them until she comes back within the week to see them.

When she got back home, she was greeted with a noisy exchange of words. It was her sister and her mother that where quarreling. Her mother was shouting on her sister saying: "As old as you are, you still can't find anything useful to do with your life. Shame on you that although you are almost 40, no man is interested in you, yet you are still under my roof eating." Then her sister replied telling her: "Are you not the one that ruined my life, forcing me to be using myself to make money for you? You never allowed me to focus on building myself. Now that I'm facing the consequences, you are heaping blame on me. Mom, you are evil!" These exchange of words made Itohan so tired because she did not know how to intervene. She simply ignore them and went inside to reason out the best way to approach this issue between her sister and her mom.   She called her mother aside later in the evening and told her that she will be leaving very early the next day, that she want to discuss something with her before she leaves. Her mother told her to go ahead. Starting from when they where in the village, Itohan narrated to her mother how she, her sister and her brother where always there for each other. She told her mother that if she had played her motherly role well, the distance between her and her sister wouldn't have been there, and that her sister's life wouldn't have turned out the way it is today. She openly told her mother that she is to be blamed for whatever challenges her sister may be facing. She told her not to use such words on her again so that she won't see herself as a failure and go into depression. Her mother thank her and promise not to exchange such words with her again.

Itohan also went to her sister to reassure her that she isn't a failure. That she can always start again to build a fine reputation for herself after she travel out of that vicinity. She thanked Itohan and express deep appreciation to her because, despite all that she and their mother did to her, she still came back to help them. Itohan reassured her that all those where in the past, that they should focus on the present and way forward. After that they had a nice time together, discussing together well into the night before they went to bed.

When her marriage day came, everybody where on ground to give her out in marriage to Raymond who came from a well respected family. Her principal was there standing for her as her father. Her mother, her sister and her brother where around and gorgeously dressed. Efe who is now married came with his wife. Her friend Juliet and many of her former classmates grace the occasion. High personalities from her organization and VIPs from the political space came too. Even some friends she made overseas came and those who couldn't make it sent greetings along with gift. It was a really delightful and happy occasion for all, especially for the newly weds. At the end of the occasion, her father was called to give her daughter and everyone his parting advice. Her principal who was standing as her father took the mic. Addressing everyone first he said: "My daughter whom we are celebrating today literally went from grass to grace. Her story should teach everyone that once there is life, there is hope. No one should give up under any heavy burden life may subject you under. If you can't carry it, roll it along, don't stop, one day you will get to your desired destination. It doesn't matter who get there first." To the newly wedded couple he said: "My beloved ones, marriage is a journey. If you walk it with understanding patience and forgiveness, you will surely go very far in it. I pray that my God should be with you both in this journey you are starting today. Don't fail to seek advice when the going is getting tough. May we gather like this to celebrate your 1st, 2nd, 10th and up to your 50th anniversary." With that, prayers where offered and the occasion was declared officially closed. Itohan and her husband continue to live an exemplary life and they came to be loved by everyone who knows them.

About The Author

Eigbe Osemudiamen Moses is someone who loves writing. He loves telling stories. This book is his first writen fiction. It was writen out of a desire to tell a story that can give moral lessons and values while entertaining the reader at the same time. He is a university graduate, and has experience in translation work.

Books By This Author

<u>NIGERIA PIDGIN AT A GLANCE</u> Anyone can use this book to learn Nigeria pidgin, even those that are foreign to the language, because everything inside is laid out side by side with its English equivalent. Even persons that do not have anyone to guild them through the learning process would find it easy. The book is clear, simple and straight to the point.

<u>PASSIVE INCOME WITH AMAZON KDP</u> Publishing books on Amazon KDP is one way to make money online passively. Many people have been cashing out big by simply publishing books here for free. But other persons are finding it difficult to start, probably because they don't have someone that will guide them through the process. By means of this book, I want to take you by the hand and guild you through the process step by step. So come along by getting a copy for yourself and start your journey of a life time passive income.